DOUBLE - AXEL DOUBT

BY JAKE MADDOX

text by Emma Carlson Berne

illustrated by Pulsar Studio
(Beehive)

Jake Maddox books are published by Stone Arch Books
A Capstone Imprint
1710 Roe Crest Drive
North Mankato, Minnesota 56003
www.capstonepub.com

*Library of Congress Cataloging-in-Publication Data is available on
the Library of Congress website.*

ISBN: 978-1-4342-2499-6 (library binding)

Summary: Gabby's new skating coach doesn't care when Gabby
says she can't do difficult jumps. Gabby has to decide if she should
follow her coach or stand
up for herself.

Art Director/Graphic Designer: Kay Fraser
Production Specialist: Michelle Biedscheid

Printed in China by Nordica.
0114/CA21400080
012014   007961R

TABLE OF CONTENTS

CHAPTER 1

THE BIG NEWS

"Now, the sit spin!" Coach Stone called from the side of the ice rink. Out on the ice, Gabby skated in a wide circle. The ice spread out before her like a sheet of glass.

Gabby sped up as she completed the circle. Her skates scraped across the smooth surface of ice.

Then she bent her knees and twirled, crouching low on the ice. She extended one leg out in front of her as she spun.

Gabby rose, still spinning, until she was upright again. She lifted her leg out behind her and glided into a backward circle to complete the move.

"Nice work, Gabby!" Coach Stone called. She motioned her student over. "Let's take a quick break from practice. I need to talk to you about something."

Gabby skated over to the side of the rink. She quickly slipped on her skate guards and sat down next to her coach in the stands. "What's going on, Coach?" she asked.

Coach Stone put her hand on Gabby's knee. "Gabby, how long have I been your coach?" she asked.

"Um . . ." Gabby paused. "Seven years," she said. "Ever since I started skating."

"Well, pretty soon we're going to have to make some changes," Coach Stone said. "I'm retiring at the end of the month." She smiled gently at Gabby. "I know this is a surprise, but I've been coaching for a long time. I'm ready for a break."

Gabby stared at her coach. She tried to understand what she had just heard. "So, does this mean you won't be my coach anymore?" she asked.

Her fingers pinched at the knees of her warm-ups. Gabby had never skated with any other coach. She wouldn't know what to do without Coach Stone.

Coach Stone nodded. "That's right," she told Gabby gently. "And even though I know it doesn't feel that way right now, I think this could be a good thing."

Gabby shook her head. *I'm not going to cry*, she told herself. But she could feel the tears filling her eyes. "How can this be a good thing?" she asked.

Coach Stone paused. "You won a lot of medals when you were younger, Gabby," she said. "But how many have you won in the past couple of years?"

Gabby thought. "Um . . . one. That third place two years ago," she said. She sat for a minute, thinking. "Wow. That's not very many."

"Exactly," Coach Stone agreed. She leaned over so that she could look into Gabby's eyes. "You need a change. You're stuck in the same place lately, and that's why you haven't been winning. Sometimes, people just need a little push forward. I think you could you use that push now."

She rose from the bench and walked over to her bag on a nearby table. She pulled out a piece of paper and handed it to Gabby as she sat back down on the bench.

Gabby unfolded the paper and gazed down at it. It read, *Coach Pearce, Rosemont Ice Arena, 555-2034*. "Who's Coach Pearce?" Gabby asked.

Coach Stone smiled. "She's the best figure-skating coach in the area," she said. "Well, until I officially retire, she's the second-best. I think she would be great as your new teacher. Coach Pearce has a different way of teaching than I do. That change might be just what you need to start winning again."

Gabby stared down at the wrinkled piece of paper.

"Gabby," Coach Stone said gently, "if you want to work with Coach Pearce, you'll have to start doing the big jumps again. Your injury is healed."

Gabby stared down at her lap. She had hurt her ankle last year when she fell doing a double Axel. Since that day, she'd only done easy, basic jumps — nothing like she used to do. She just couldn't make herself.

Her ankle was healed now, but every time she flung herself in the air, the memory of her fall came rushing back. It was just too scary.

Coach Stone had been understanding. They had worked on spins, footwork, and easy jumps for the past year. Gabby had avoided big jumps — like Axels, Lutzes, and flips. Coach Stone said she was ready, but Gabby just couldn't do it.

The black writing on the paper in Gabby's hand blurred. Her eyes overflowed. A big tear fell right on the paper. "I don't want to skate with anyone but you," she whispered.

Coach Stone smiled and pulled Gabby into a hug. "I know. Leaving my students is the hardest thing I've ever done," she said. "But all things have to change. And you do, too. Just give Coach Pearce a try. She might be good for you."

"Maybe . . ." Gabby said doubtfully. She wasn't sure. How could anyone replace Coach Stone?

CHAPTER 2

MEETING THE COACH

After dinner that night, Gabby excused herself and went to her room. She took out the piece of paper Coach Stone had given her and stared at it. Finally, she sighed, picked up the phone, and dialed the number.

A sharp voice answered after two rings. "Hello?"

"Hi, this is Gabby Lange," Gabby said nervously. "Um, Coach Stone —"

"Ah, yes," Coach Pearce cut in, not giving Gabby time to finish. "Coach Stone told me you would be calling. I want you to audition for me. Tomorrow at Rosemont Arena. That's where we practice. Don't be late."

Gabby opened her mouth to reply, but instead, she heard a *click*. Coach Pearce had hung up the phone. The dial tone beeped in Gabby's ear.

Slowly, she set the phone down. Tomorrow was awfully soon for an audition. She didn't even have time to prepare.

But what choice did she have? Coach Pearce didn't seem like the kind of coach you argued with.

* * *

The next afternoon, Gabby made her way into Rosemont Arena. She'd never been to the modern ice rink before. It was brand new, all glass and shiny metal. It was so different than the old arena where she skated with Coach Stone. As she stood in front of the big glass doors, trying to find the courage to push them open, someone bumped into her from behind.

"Oh!" Gabby exclaimed, stumbling forward a few steps before catching herself. She turned around to see a boy about her own age.

"Whoa! Sorry about that," the boy said. "Are you okay?"

She looked him over as she brushed her hair back out of her face. "Yeah, I'm fine," she said. "Thanks."

"Are you lost?" he asked. "This place is huge. It took me weeks to find my way around."

Gabby shook her head. "I think I'll be okay," she said. "Thanks, though." She hitched her skating bag a little higher on her shoulder. The boy smiled at her and pushed through the big doors, disappearing inside.

Gabby took a deep breath, trying to calm her shaky stomach. Maybe Coach Pearce wouldn't expect big jumps today. It was just an audition, after all. *There's nothing to be nervous about,* Gabby told herself.

She shoved open the glass doors. Inside, skating banners hung from the high ceiling. Skaters lounged on benches lining the walls.

Straight ahead, Gabby could see the entrance to the main rink. The shouts of coaches and the scrape of skates filtered through the heavy doors. One woman's gruff voice rose above the rest.

Maybe that's Coach Pearce, Gabby thought. *I guess there's only one way to find out.* She pulled open the doors and felt a cool blast of air on her face.

The ice was covered with skaters practicing jumps and spins. Their coaches shouted directions from the sidelines. "Ah, Gabrielle!" a small woman cried. Her voice echoed in the vast rink. The woman strode toward Gabby, holding out both of her hands.

"Hello," Gabby said, shaking the woman's hand. "Thanks for meeting me."

"Gladly!" Coach Pearce cried, hurrying over to the sidelines, where a small table was set up. "Coach Stone told me you're an excellent skater. It's too bad she's retiring, but I think this could be a very good opportunity for you."

Coach Pearce picked up a piece of paper from the table. "Now, Coach Stone mentioned that you haven't done any complex jumps for almost a year now. But she tells me your old injury is perfectly healed," she said with a smile. "I'm sure you're a lovely jumper. I'm excited to see what you can do today."

Gabby felt the blood drain from her face. "Today? I-I don't know if I can," she stammered. She imagined the thud of her body hitting the ice. She stepped back. "I'm not sure this is a good idea," she said.

Coach Pearce put down the piece of paper and fixed Gabby with a stern gaze. "How many medals have you won in the past year, Gabrielle?" she asked.

Gabby looked down at the toes of her boots. "None," she mumbled.

Coach Pearce nodded. "That's right," she said. "And that is because you have not performed any high-level jumps, correct?"

Gabby didn't respond. She focused on her shoelaces.

Coach Pearce was silent for a moment. Then she sighed. "All right, Gabrielle," she said. "You will skate for me today with only small jumps. For now."

Gabby looked up, a grin splitting across her face. "Thank you," she said. Coach Pearce nodded, a little smile on her lips.

CHAPTER 3
THE AUDITION

Gabby sat down on a bench at the side of the ice. She quickly pulled off her boots and laced up her skates. She tugged the familiar laces tight and stood up, bending to touch her toes. She felt her calves and hamstrings stretch and loosen.

She straightened up. Her body felt strong, warm, and loose. She skated onto the shining ice, her arms swinging by her sides.

It's going to be fine, she told herself. *It's just a normal routine . . . I've done this a thousand times.*

Behind her, Coach Pearce clapped her hands. The sound echoed like a rifle shot in the big space.

"All right, Gabrielle, please begin," she said. "Let's get you warmed up. I want you to start with an upright spin, then a sit spin."

Quietly, Gabby skated in a large circle, warming up her legs. She could feel Coach Pearce watching her. If she skated well, Coach Pearce would take her on as a student. And if she didn't . . .

I'll be walking right back out those glass doors, Gabby thought. *And I don't want that. I want to skate.*

As Coach Pearce watched, Gabby sped up and moved into a layback spin. She gracefully arched her back and let her head drop back behind her. She extended her arms overhead, spinning so fast the arena blurred around her.

She slowly came to a halt. "Very nice!" Coach Pearce called. Gabby felt a little prick of pride in her chest. "Please continue."

Her heart pumping harder now, Gabby skated backward around the edge of the arena, holding her arms out by her sides. She pivoted lightly on her skates and turned to face forward again.

Next, she moved across the ice on the diagonal. Gabby crossed her legs, one over the other, turning forward, then backward, then forward again.

She glanced quickly at Coach Pearce. The coach had her hands on her hips, smiling as she watched. Smoothly, Gabby rose and began a layback spin, letting her arms and head fall gracefully back behind her.

"Excellent, Gabrielle!" Coach Pearce called. "Now let me see a single toe loop."

That was a little jump. Gabby skated backward to gather speed. She stuck her left toe pick into the ice and pushed herself into the air.

Gabby rotated a half turn in the air before landing on her right skate, arms held slightly out to her sides as she glided backward. Then, from across the arena, she heard Coach Pearce shout, "Now a double Axel! Now, Gabrielle!"

Without thinking, Gabby turned and spread her arms to prepare for the jump. Then she realized what she was doing. A double Axel was a top-level jump. A skater had to take off from the forward outside edge of one skate and land on the back outside edge of the opposite foot. Gabby would have to rotate a full two and a half times in the air to complete the jump.

Gabby screeched to a halt. Standing in the middle of the rink, panting, she stared at Coach Pearce. Her coach gazed back, her eyes calm and knowing.

"You said no big jumps," Gabby said. Her voice was nervous.

Coach Pearce shrugged. "I wanted to see if you could do it if you didn't think about it first," she said.

She looked down at her clipboard and made a mark. "You're going to have to get over your fear, Gabrielle. Jumps are a part of a skater's life." Her voice was hard. "You're an excellent skater. I'll take you on as my student." Without waiting for a reply, Coach Pearce turned her back and walked away.

"That will be all," she called back over her shoulder. "Be here at three o'clock tomorrow. And Gabby . . . don't be late."

Gabby stood frozen in the middle of the ice, arms at her sides, mouth hanging open. She watched Coach Pearce walk through a door at the other end of the rink and disappear.

Looks like I have a new coach, Gabby thought, *whether I like it or not.*

CHAPTER 4
UP TO THE TASK

The next afternoon, Gabby made sure she was at the rink on time. As she pushed open the big doors, she immediately spotted Coach Pearce, bundled in her huge puffy parka.

"Hello, Coach Pearce," Gabby said as she walked over.

Coach Pearce pointed at the bench in front of her. "Sit, Gabrielle," she commanded.

"Uh, actually, I prefer Gabby," Gabby said. She hadn't wanted to correct Coach Pearce the day before, but now that she was officially her student, it was probably okay.

"Please don't interrupt, Gabrielle," Coach Pearce said.

Gabby's eyes widened. Coach Pearce definitely had a different style of coaching than Coach Stone. Gabby sat still on the bench, her back very straight as she listened.

Coach Pearce paced in front of her. "I have some ideas for you, Gabrielle," she explained. "As you may know, the regional competition is coming up in just a couple of weeks. I think you could do very well if you practice hard enough."

She paused and stared at Gabby. "We'll focus on footwork and spins. For now, your jumps will be a single flip, a single toe loop, and a single Salchow," she said. "I'm sure you can handle that."

Gabby nodded. *All of those jumps are easy, little ones*, she thought with relief. Coach Pearce hadn't mentioned any high-level jumps, like the double Axel. *I wonder why*, Gabby thought. She didn't have time to think about it more, though. Coach Pearce was already shooing her toward the ice to begin her warm-up.

* * *

Gabby had never skated as hard as she did during the next two weeks. She was drenched in sweat at the end of every practice. Every day, she worked on her routine for the regional competition.

Some of the moves were hard, especially the flying spin, which she'd never done before. But Gabby was pleased that she hadn't had any trouble so far. She'd even done a slightly harder jump — a single Axel.

Coach Pearce hadn't said anything about doing a high-level jump since the audition. Gabby tried to forget about it. But in her heart, she knew she would have to do at least one double jump to compete at the juvenile level. Still, every time that thought came up, she shoved it aside. Coach Pearce was the coach — she knew what she was doing.

CHAPTER 5

THE NEW JUMP

A week before the competition, Gabby had worked through most of her routine. Only the ending was left, and Coach Pearce still hadn't told her what she would do.

For more than two hours, Gabby skated through the beginning and middle of her routine over and over. She was completely exhausted. Finally, Coach Pearce called out, "Excellent work, Gabrielle! Two-minute break."

Gabby bent over, rested her hands on her knees, and panted. Coach Pearce was really pushing her today. At this rate, she'd definitely be ready for Saturday.

She stood up and took a gulp from her water bottle. Then she skated to the center of the rink where Coach Pearce stood waiting for her.

"Let's run through the routine one more time," her coach said, placing her hands on her hips. "But this time, I want you to do the ending. Please finish with a double Axel." Her voice was firm. "This is an important jump. If you can land it, it could help you win."

Gabby's stomach dropped. She'd known this moment was going to come. She'd been avoiding it as long as she could.

"I've watched you skate for two weeks now," Coach Pearce said. "You can do this. Your ankle is fine. Your single Axel is solid. It's time to take it back to the level you were at before your injury."

Gabby swallowed. "I don't know, Coach Pearce," she said. "What if I'm not ready? Can't I just do the single Axel instead?"

Coach Pearce looked startled. "Excuse me?" she asked in shock. "I've been coaching for twenty years. Do you think you know better than me?"

Gabby's mouth felt dry. She'd never argued with a coach before. She shook her head. "No. I'm sorry," she muttered.

Coach Pearce stood back. "Then please do the jump," she said. Gabby could tell that she didn't really have a choice.

Gabby took a deep breath. Maybe she was worrying too much. After all, Coach Pearce was her coach. And she'd done the single Axel just fine. She just had to do the double without thinking.

Gabby skated in a large warm-up circle around the outside of the rink. Then she nodded at Coach Pearce to show that she was ready.

Coach Pearce started the music. Gabby closed her eyes, trying to feel the rhythm she would need. Fear started to creep through her, but she tried to keep her mind blank.

Don't think, she told herself. *Just don't think.* She neared the center of the rink and moved into a toe loop followed by a sit spin.

Gabby swung her body around and began skating backward around the ice. She increased her speed — faster and then faster again. She hadn't skated this fast since the day of the fall. Gabby could feel her pulse pounding. The music grew louder and faster.

"Now!" Coach Pearce shouted. "Double Axel, now!"

Gabby bent her knees and stretched her arms out to her sides. She pushed off the ice hard, launching her body into the air. She drew her arms into her body, and for a moment, her heart soared as she spun through the air.

Then her right skate tangled with her left. She felt herself coming out of the air much too quickly.

Falling, her mind screamed. *Falling*. She didn't have time to unwind her body. The ice seemed to rise up to meet her. She fell with a thud, landing on her side.

Gabby gasped, trying to breathe, but the fall had knocked the wind out of her. She lay on the ice for a few moments, trying not to panic.

As soon as she was able to breathe again she raised herself onto her hands and knees, her head down. In the corner of the arena, Coach Pearce stopped the music, and silence filled the ring.

CHAPTER 6

DO YOU WANT TO WIN?

It had happened again. Another hard jump, another hard fall. Shakily, Gabby stood up. She brushed ice off her warm-up tights. She felt sick to her stomach.

Coach Pearce walked over. "Are you all right, Gabrielle?" she asked.

Coach Pearce checked Gabby's neck and shoulders for injuries. "Turn your head," she ordered. Silently, Gabby turned her head side to side.

Coach Pearce felt Gabby's arms and ankles. "Nothing broken," she said. She walked back to the side of the ring and turned the music back on. "Start again, please. Toe loop, sit spin, double Axel."

Gabby panicked. She couldn't try the double Axel again. Her mind raced. *What if I fall again? What if I get hurt again?* She stood, frozen, in the middle of the ice.

"Did you hear me?" Coach Pearce asked. "Begin the routine again."

Gabby still didn't move. Coach Pearce came toward her. Her gaze was intense. "What is going on here?" she demanded.

Gabby drew in her breath. "I'm so sorry, Coach Pearce," she managed to say. "I can't do the jump again." She stared down at the scuffed toes of her skates.

"And why is that?" Coach Pearce asked.

Gabby swallowed. "I, um, don't feel like I'm ready for that hard of a jump," she said. "If it's okay with you, I'll just do the single Axel."

Coach Pearce shook her head. "I'm afraid that is not going to be good enough," she said. "You'll never be a winner if you won't do the double. Single won't cut it."

Gabby bit her lip.

Coach Pearce came close and put a hand on Gabby's shoulder, looking directly into her face. "You can do this jump," Coach Pearce said. "It's nerves that are getting in your way, not skill. Look, do you want to win?"

"Yes," Gabby almost whispered.

"Then you will do the jump," Coach Pearce said. She turned and walked to the side of the arena.

"Practice is over for today," she called over her shoulder. "Be ready to do the double Axel tomorrow morning."

Outside, the fresh air felt cold on Gabby's face. She walked home slowly, avoiding the puddles on the sidewalk. Her feet felt heavy as she climbed the front steps of her house.

Her mind was filled with images of Coach Pearce's angry face and herself, crumpled on the ice. Suddenly, another image filled her mind — herself twirling in the air, arms drawn in close, then landing the double Axel perfectly as the crowd cheered.

Gabby walked upstairs to her quiet room and sank down on the bed, burying her face in her hands. She sat that way for a long time, trying to decide what she should do.

Several minutes later, Gabby raised her head. Coach Stone would know what to do. *Just because she's not my coach anymore doesn't mean she can't still help me out,* Gabby thought.

She reached over and grabbed her cell phone from the bedside table. She scrolled through the numbers in her phone until she found the one she was looking for and dialed.

"Hello?" an unfamiliar voice answered.

"Um, hello, is this Coach Stone?" Gabby asked.

"I'm sorry, this is her sister," the woman answered. "Coach Stone left this morning for a cruise to the Bahamas. She'll be back at the end of the month. Can I take a message?"

Gabby sank back on her pillows in disappointment. She'd been counting on Coach Stone.

"Hello?" the woman said. "Hello?"

"Never mind," Gabby muttered. She slowly clicked the phone shut. "Looks like I'm on my own now," she said to the empty room.

CHAPTER 7
GABBY'S DECISION

Gabby barely slept that night. She felt like the night would never end. She twisted in her sweaty sheets, turning her pillow over again and again to find a cool spot. Finally, near dawn, she fell into a restless sleep.

When her alarm went off at eight, she opened her eyes. Her mind was finally made up. She needed to talk to Coach Pearce.

After climbing out of bed, Gabby walked to the bathroom. She stepped under the pounding spray of the shower. She knew she'd have to hurry if she wanted to catch Coach Pearce before practice.

Gabby jogged all the way to the ice rink. When she arrived, she tugged open the big front doors and stepped inside. This early, the rink was practically empty.

Instead of going to the ice, she headed to the long hallway on the side of the arena where all the coaches had their offices. The door on the end read "Margaret Pearce." Gabby raised her hand and knocked.

"Come in," Coach Pearce called.

Gabby pushed open the door. Coach Pearce sat behind a desk piled high with papers. She was scowling at a clipboard.

When she looked up, her face broke into a smile. "Ah, Gabrielle," she said. "I thought I might be seeing you this morning. Ready to work on that double Axel?"

Gabby's heart was pounding. "Actually, that's what I wanted to talk to you about," she replied. "I've decided the double Axel is too much for me right now. I'm excited to do the rest of the routine, but I won't be doing the double Axel," she said. "I'm happy to do the single, though."

Her voice sounded stronger than she felt. She swallowed hard and forced herself to look Coach Pearce in the face.

Coach Pearce frowned. "I told you. You can't compete at the juvenile level without the double. There's no point," she replied.

"I'm sorry," Gabby said quietly. "I just don't feel like I'm ready to do the jump. If that means I have to compete at a lower level, then I'm okay with that."

Coach Pearce raised her eyebrows. "I'm surprised," she said. "I must say, I've never had a skater refuse a jump before."

Gabby swallowed hard but forced herself to stand up straight. "I'm really sorry. I've been up practically all night thinking about this. I'll admit it — I am afraid to do the double Axel. I had a really bad experience jumping last year. Even if it's just my nerves, and not my skill, I need more practice with the double before I can do it in competition."

Gabby and Coach Pearce stared at each other. The only sound in the room was the loud ticking of the wall clock.

Gabby held her breath. What if Coach Pearce wouldn't listen? What if she dropped her as a student? Finally, the coach sighed.

"You're right," she said. "I may have been a coach for thirty years, but I still get excited when I see a skater with a lot of talent — like you. Maybe my excitement got in the way of my common sense. I shouldn't have pushed you so hard on something you don't feel ready for."

Gabby breathed a sigh of relief. "Thank you!" she exclaimed. "Thank you for understanding." Her whole body felt lighter than it had for the past two weeks.

Coach Pearce continued, "We'll practice the double together for the future. For now, I'm putting you down for the pre-juvenile level at the competition. You'll do the single Axel, and we'll go from there."

She picked up her clipboard and made a note. "Don't be late tomorrow," she added. "Eight o'clock at the arena. The event begins at nine-thirty, and you will skate at ten."

"I'll be there," Gabby promised.

CHAPTER 8

THE AXEL

Gabby hardly recognized the ice arena when she arrived the next morning. The backstage area, which was usually empty, was packed with dozens of skaters. Coaches in shiny warm-up outfits talked to their students in the corners, while proud parents snapped picture after picture.

Gabby dumped her skate bag in a corner. Then she went over to check out the audience.

A wall separated the backstage from the ice. Gabby peered over it and gasped. The bleachers were packed with parents, siblings, and grandparents. Some people were even standing up at the back. Gabby could feel the excitement all around her.

The three judges sat at their long, high table with their scorecards in front of them. Gabby's heart sped up.

The first skater was already on the ice. Gabby watched as the music began. *She must be an intermediate skater,* Gabby thought. She watched the girl perform a perfect triple Lutz. The audience loved it.

Gabby was filled with doubt. She wanted to be out there doing jumps that made the audience gasp and clap, just like they were doing now. *Maybe I should be doing the double Axel,* she thought.

Gabby spun around when someone touched her shoulder. Coach Pearce stood behind her, bundled in her usual parka. She smiled. "Ready for your performance, Gabrielle?" she asked.

Gabby looked around and then drew her coach into a quiet corner. "I don't know. I'm rethinking things," she said. "Is it too late to move me into the juvenile competition? Maybe I should try the double. What do you think?" she asked, looking nervously at her coach's face.

To her surprise, Coach Pearce shook her head. "No," she said firmly, picking up Gabby's skate bag. "Come on, you need to warm up. You're next."

"No?" Gabby repeated, hurrying after her coach.

Coach Pearce turned around. "No," she said again. "You were right yesterday. There will be many, many more competitions for you, Gabrielle. You'll have many, many chances to perform the double Axel. Today, skate and enjoy yourself. The single Axel will be enough."

Coach Pearce smiled for an instant. Then her face returned to its usual frown. "Enough talking!" she snapped. "Time to warm up!"

* * *

The announcer's voice boomed over the arena. "Gabrielle Lange!"

The audience grew quiet. Gabby gave her coach one last glance. Coach Pearce nodded and made a shooing motion with her hands. *Go*, she mouthed.

Gabby took a deep breath and stepped onto the ice. The minute her skates touched the slick surface, she relaxed. It had been so long since she'd competed and even longer since she'd felt good about her routine.

She skated smoothly to the center of the ice and got into position. Her stomach felt calm. Her mind was clear. She knew exactly what she was going to do.

At a signal from the head judge, the music began. Gabby swept into her first move, the sit spin. Crouching close to the ice, she spun quickly, tracing perfectly round circles on the ice beneath her blade.

Gabby spun into an edge spiral next, her right leg out behind her and her arms held out to her sides. She could feel the sweat rolling down her back, despite the cold air of the rink.

She spun easily on one skate. The audience cheered as she finished her spin and glided across the rink.

Gabby moved into the position for the Axel. She skated backward, her head turned, her arms held out next to her. She felt her skates moving faster. Then it was time.

She threw herself into the air, rotating a full turn and a half, holding her arms close to her body. Gabby felt herself soaring in the air. She knew that the jump was perfect.

She landed lightly on one foot, the other extended behind her as she glided backward. At the same time, she heard the audience cheer. Gabby let the applause wash over her.

Gabby swept into her closing position, arms lifted over her head. She looked to the right.

The judges were nodding and smiling at one another. Gabby broke into a smile, too. She barely felt her skates touch the ice as she skated off.

Coach Pearce was waiting for her. "Well?" Gabby asked nervously. "What did you think?" She slipped the blade covers onto her skates.

Coach Pearce didn't say anything. She draped a jacket around Gabby's shoulders and led her to the bench to wait for her scores.

Gabby's heart dropped. Had she been wrong? Should she have done the double after all?

Then Coach Pearce finally spoke. "Well, it was only a single, Gabrielle," she said. "But it was the best single I've seen in a long time. And that is because you skated with confidence. The judges will agree."

She pointed to the scoreboard over the ring. The crowd cheered as the score flashed: *Gabrielle Lange, Pre-Juvenile, 9.0.*

Gabby squealed and threw her arms around Coach Pearce. That was her highest score yet! Coach Pearce smiled and patted Gabby's back firmly. "Very good work," she said. "I can't wait to see what you can do next."

ABOUT THE AUTHOR

Emma Carlson Berne has written more than a dozen books for children and young adults, including teen romance novels, biographies, and history books. She lives in Cincinnati, Ohio with her husband, Aaron, her son, Henry, and her dog, Holly.

ABOUT THE ILLUSTRATOR

Pulsar Studio is a collection of artists from Argentina who work to bring editorial projects to life. They work with companies from different parts of the world designing characters, short stories for children, textbooks, art for book covers, comics, licensed art, and more. Images are their means of expression.

GLOSSARY

arena (uh-REE-nuh)—a large area that is used for sports or entertainment

audition (aw-DISH-uhn)—a short performance to see whether someone is suitable for a part in a play, concert, etc.

competition (kom-puh-TISH-uhn)—a contest of some kind

complex (kom-PLEKS)—very complicated

intense (in-TENSS)—showing stong feelings

intermediate (in-tur-MEE-dee-it)—a higher than juvenile level of competition

juvenile (JOO-vuh-nile)—one of the levels of competition in figure skating

retire (ri-TIRE)—to give up work, usually because of old age

routine (roo-TEEN)—a regular way or pattern of doing things

scuff (SKUHF)—to scratch or scrape something and leave a mark

DISCUSSION QUESTIONS

1. Gabby didn't want to perform difficult jumps, even though her coach thought it was a good idea. Who do you think was right, Gabby or Coach Pearce? Talk about the different viewpoints.

2. What would you do if you were in Gabby's situation? Discuss some other ways Gabby could have reacted and what you would have done if you were her.

3. Gabby was injured while performing a difficult skating jump. Have you ever been injured while playing a sport? Talk about it.

WRITING PROMPTS

1. Gabby had to make a major change when she got a new coach. Have you ever had to make a big change? What happened? How did you react? Write about it.

2. Do you think Gabby was right to stand up to her coach? Have you ever had to stand up to an adult for something you believed in? Write about that experience.

3. Gabby was afraid to try harder jumps because of her injury. Have you ever been nervous about trying something? Write about how you overcame your fear.

MORE ABOUT FIGURE SKATING JUMPS

Jumps are a major part of figure skating competitions. Below, in order of easiest to most difficult, are the six most common jumps:

Salchow: This edge jump was named for Ulrich Salchow, who first performed it in 1909. The takeoff is done on the back inside edge of one skate. It is landed on the back outside edge of the other skate after one or more rotations.

Toe loop: This is one of the simplest toe jumps. It begins with a toe pick and requires a skater to take off and land on the back outside edge of the same skate.

Loop: A loop jump requires a skater to take off from a back outside edge, do a full rotation in the air, and land on the same back outside edge used to take off. This is an "edge jump" since no toe assist is needed to take off. It's often the second part of a combination.

Flip: This toe jump begins with a skater on a back inside edge. The skater then does a toe pick with the other foot, jumps a full revolution, and lands on the back outside edge of the opposite foot.

Lutz: The Lutz is named for Austrian skater Alois Lutz, who first performed it in 1913. This is a toe jump similar to a flip jump. The only difference is that the takeoff is from a back outside edge, rather than a back inside edge.

Axel: Named for Axel Paulsen, who performed it in 1882, the Axel is the most difficult jump. It's an edge jump that takes off on a forward outside edge and lands on the back outside edge of the opposite foot. A skater must make one and a half revolutions while in the air.

MORE Fabulou Sports BOOKS

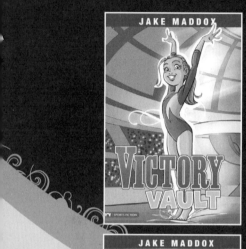

JAKE MADDOX

VICTORY VAULT

JAKE MADDOX

CHEER CAPTAIN

JAKE MADDOX

Drive to the HOOP

JAKE MADDOX

JUMP SERVE

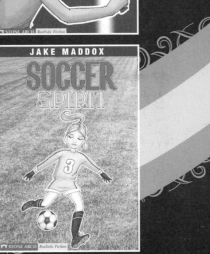